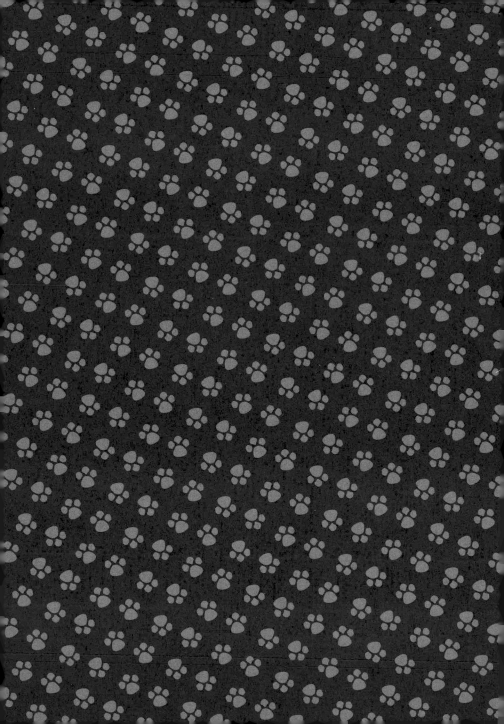

HELPER HOUNDS
Louis

Helps Ajani Fight Racism

Dedication
To Megan and Jennifer of Peace for Pits.
Thanks for helping our boy find his way home to us.

HELPER HOUNDS

Louis

Helps Ajani Fight Racism

Caryn Rivadeneira
Illustrated by Priscilla Alpaugh

RED CHAIR ·PRESS·

Egremont, Massachusetts

RED CHAIR PRESS
BOOKS FOR YOUNG READERS

www.redchairpress.com

 Free educator's guide at www.redchairpress.com/free-resources

Publisher's Cataloging-In-Publication Data

Names: Rivadeneira, Caryn Dahlstrand, author. | Alpaugh, Priscilla, illustrator. | Rivadeneira, Caryn Dahlstrand. Helper hounds.

Title: Louis helps Ajani fight racism / Caryn Rivadeneira ; illustrated by Priscilla Alpaugh.

Description: Egremont, Massachusetts: Red Chair Press, [2021] | Includes fun facts and information about the dog breed, Standard poodle. | Summary: Ajani loves having a dad from Denmark and a mom from Jamaica. Ajani speaks three languages and gets to spend summers with his grandparents in the coolest places. But when a classmate overhears dark-skinned Ajani speaking Danish, the boy makes a hurtful, racist comment. Ajani is crushed. Until a chance encounter with Louis the Helper Hound helps Ajani feel proud of his heritage and helps him and his classmates fight racism"--Provided by publisher.

Identifiers: ISBN 9781643710860 (hardcover) | ISBN 9781643710877 (softcover) | ISBN 9781643710884 (ebook)

Subjects: LCSH: Standard poodle--Juvenile fiction. | Racially mixed families--Juvenile fiction. | Racism--Juvenile fiction. | CYAC: Dogs--Fiction. | Racially mixed families--Fiction. | Racism--Fiction.

Classification: LCC PZ7.1.R57627 Lo 2021 (print) | LCC PZ7.1.R57627 (ebook) | DDC [E]--dc23

Library of Congress Control Number: 20202948980

Photos: iStock

Printed in the United States of America

0421 1P CGF21

CHAPTER 1

I did a double-take.

A shaggy dog stared at me through the window. I turned my snout to the left and then to the right. The shaggy dog turned with me! I woofed my smallest woof at the huge, curly-headed dog. The dog woofed back, but I couldn't hear it.

Behind me, Mrs. Tramill laughed. "Louis, who do you think you are woofing at? You're too smart to fall for that!"

Wait a minute… Was that goofy-looking guy *me*?

I tilted my head. The dog in the window followed.

I shoved my tongue out. The dog did the same.

That floofy-faced fellow *was* me.

Thank goodness I was standing on the grooming table at Mrs. Tramill's Poodle Grooming Salon. Lisa had really let me go. Sure, Lisa had been really busy at work, but this was ridiculous. Good thing, I looked adorable in my shaggy "puppy cut."

But still. This was silly. I was a Helper Hound! We had standards! Well, at least I did. I was a standard poodle after all. My friends Penny and Sparky, King Tut and Spooky, may not care much about their looks. But let's face it: how they looked didn't affect what they could do. Our fancy haircuts help us standard poodles do our jobs. Besides making me look handsome, my smooth snout, properly placed poofs, and fluffy cuffs are there to keep me warm and help me float. And you never know

when a Helper
Hound is going
to need to jump
in some
cold water.

Speaking of
water. *Spritz.*
Spritz. Spritz.

Mrs. Tramill
sprayed my hair with
her special "poodle mix
spray" and combed through
my fluff.

"It has been far too long since I've seen you,
Louis," she said. "You haven't even heard the
latest…"

Mrs. Tramill loved to talk while she trimmed
my hair. She'd catch me up on all the dog
news. She would tell me all about which dogs
failed obedience classes, which got a little too

snappy, and which dogs were putting on a little too much winter weight. I didn't really care what she had to say, but I did like to hear Mrs. Tramill talk. Her voice was very soothing. And she knew a lot—about the dogs in town, but also, about the world.

"I *did* go to Harvard," Mrs. Tramill told everyone—whether they asked or not.

Mrs. Tramill would giggle as she said it, but the tagline on her website and business cards said: BEST-EDUCATED DOG GROOMER IN THE WORLD.

"Oh, people think I'm showing off," she would say. "But I hate it when people *assume* things about me, you know? I love to surprise people!"

Her love of surprises is probably why she loved transforming raggedy poodles into perfectly *coiffed* (that means, hair-done) dogs.

After blowing my hair dry, Mrs. Tramill

said, "Ah, *much* better. You're a proper poodle now!"

She slid a mirror in front of me and said, "Whatcha think?"

Now that was the Louis I knew! Back to my usual amazing self. Mrs. Tramill had worked her magic and made Harvard proud—and not a moment too soon.

While I was enjoying one of Mrs. Tramill's homemade and *organic* chewies in my waiting kennel, Lisa came back to get me. Mrs. Tramill snapped open the cage and handed my leash to Lisa. I wagged and wagged. Lisa told me how handsome I looked—and how nice I smelled.

"It's the spray," Mrs. Tramill said. "I add a bit of lemon."

"Wonderful. And sorry I was late!" Lisa said. "But I got a phone call as I was leaving."

"Oh?" Mrs. Tramill said. "A new case?"

Mrs. Tramill *loved* hearing about our cases— probably so she could tell her next client all about them.

"Actually, yes!" Lisa said. "Though, it's a rough one."

"Oh, *really*," Mrs. Tramill said. Her eyebrows raised high on her face.

"This isn't something to be gossiped about," Lisa said. "These are real people, with real feelings!"

"Of course," Mrs. Tramill said. "I only repeat this stuff to the dogs."

Lisa laughed. "Of course, I can't tell you details—Helper Hounds work is private—but a boy is being teased because of his race."

Mrs. Tramill gasped. "That's horrid!"

"Yes, it is. The kids in his class laughed at him when they heard him speaking Danish. They thought it was funny to see a Black kid speaking it."

Mrs. Tramill shook her head. "That's awful. Kids can be so mean—and foolish! That child should be celebrated. He knows two languages!"

"Three, actually. His dad is from Denmark, and his mom is from Jamaica. So he speaks English, Danish, and Patois," Lisa said. "He's a real international kid!"

"I wish I could meet him. I studied languages a bit, you know, at Harvard..."

Lisa smiled and cut her off before she could continue.

"It's so hard when kids are mean," Lisa said. "I think that's why I like dogs so much!"

"Dogs don't judge or care what people look like," Mrs. Tramill said. But then her eyes drifted away. "Well, except for..."

And then Mrs. Tramill told Lisa all about Duke the miniature schnauzer—and how he barked at anyone in a baseball cap. "Just hated those things and anyone who wore them."

Lisa laughed and admitted that dogs do have their quirks too.

"But this is more than a quirk," Lisa said. "These kids really hurt the boy's feelings—and more. Assuming things or making fun of people based on their skin color is…"

"Racist," Mrs. Tramill said. "That's a terrible, hurtful thing."

Lisa nodded. "It is indeed," she said. "So we better be off. I think Louis can help this boy and his teacher help the class understand the dangers of assuming too much about others."

"You can tell them about me, the best-educated dog groomer in the world!" Mrs. Tramill bent over to fluff my neck hair. "People are best when they surprise us!"

"Or, I could tell them about what *this* guy was like when we first found him. He is full of surprises!"

"He was also full of fleas…" Mrs. Tramill said.

I sat down and scratched my shoulder with my back leg. Just the memory of the day Lisa found me made me itchy all over again.

CHAPTER 2

When Lisa found me, my
hair was as long and black
and curly as a picture of
King Louis the Fourteenth
of France. That's why she
named me Louis.

I was about as far from
being a king as a dog
can get. I spent my days wandering around
the north woods— winter, spring, summer, or
fall—looking for food or fun or someone to
love me. When it rained hard or got too cold,
I'd stay home. But I didn't like that. I lived in a

falling-down cabin with a few people who yelled at each other a lot—and never paid attention to me.

They left me some blankets in the corner and gave me their leftover food. But they never petted me or told me I was good. At least, not since the day *they* found me wandering in the woods.

They were nice to save me when I was just a scared lonely puppy with no backstory (even I can't remember where I came from). But it was like they only had one good deed in them. Loving and caring for me was too much.

So, I learned to fend for myself. In the morning, I'd head out to find water and visit the neighbor cabins. The good news was our cabin was on a huge lake filled with fresh, cold water. That lake was surrounded by other cabins that people rented during the summer. Most of the people were friendly and got used to me napping on their deck. Lots of families would put out water bowls or leftover food. Sometimes kids would pet me. Other times, parents would pull their kids away and say I was covered in ticks and fleas and burrs. And I was!

My big hair caught everything. I itched most of the time but got pretty used to it. Sometimes I'd swim in the lake to cool and clean off.

It wasn't the worst life, but it wasn't a great life. I was lonely most of the time. Every time a family was nice to me, I hoped they would invite me to hop into their minivan as they packed it up. But it never happened. Well, not until Lisa showed up with her daughter, Doe. That's when everything changed.

• • •

"Mom!" a girl yelled. "There's a *bear* on our porch."

A screen door screeched open behind me.

"Well, I'll be…" a woman said.

That woman was Lisa. The girl? That was Doe.

Lisa knelt down in front of me. I walked over for a sniff and a lick. She pushed my hair out of my eyes and said, "You're not much of a bear. I think you're a *poodle* under all this mess."

I didn't know if she was right or not about the poodle. But I knew I was a mess. I ducked my head into her chest and leaned in. It was the only way I could think to ask for help.

"Where do you live, buddy?" Lisa asked.

"It doesn't look like he *lives* anywhere," Doe said. "He's full of burrs."

"And ticks from the look of things. This guy needs help."

It worked! Lisa understood me.

Lisa shook her head and took out her phone.

Before I knew it, Lisa and Doe were hoisting me into their minivan and taking me into town. I'd never been in a car before. I'd never been to town before. It was really something! Lots of people and smells and *other dogs!* I hung my head out the window and took in everything.

I loved it. That is, until we got to the vet. No surprise: I'd never been to a vet before either.

"Ah, yes," the vet said as she looked into my

14

ears. "I've heard stories about this guy before. 'The big bear-dog in the woods.' He likes to visit the cabins."

"Does he belong to anyone?" Lisa asked.

"Yes," the vet said. "But they don't pay much attention to him."

"Obviously," Doe said. She rolled her eyes. Then petted my head and told me I was a good boy. I licked her nose. She was a good girl.

"He needs all his shots," the vet said. "And he'll need flea treatment and heartworm meds. This could get expensive. And he's not your dog..."

"Well, how do we make him our dog?" Lisa said. "I work with a rescue back home. We can find him a family that will love him. Properly."

The vet took a deep breath. "I'm not *exactly* sure where he lives," she said. "But I could guess. If I give you an address, you could visit his people and see if they're willing to let him go."

"We shouldn't even have to ask!" Doe said. "If they loved him, they'd care for him."

Lisa put her hand on Doe. "It's true," she said. "But he's still not our dog. Let's go see."

Lisa gave me a kiss on my big head. I whined when they left me behind. But another lady at the vet took me into a bath and scrubbed suds deep into my fur. It felt wonderful. Then, she toweled me off and gave me a big bowl of dog food. When she put me into a long kennel, I fell asleep on soft blankets.

I woke up to Doe asking if I thought I'd like to live in the city.

CHAPTER 3

Turns out, my people *had* been willing to let me go.

"Just took a few dollars," Doe said. "Well, actually, a *lot* of dollars. But you were worth it!"

I spent that night at the vet's. They gave me shots and *neutered* me. That means: I got a small operation so I wouldn't go around making puppies. I felt a little woozy the next morning, but when Lisa and Doe came back to get me, I had eaten, peed, and pooped. My tail was wagging and I was ready to go.

That is, until I caught a glimpse of a trim black dog looking at me through a window.

This dog had short hair, combed out to a soft fluff. This dog didn't even have one burr stuck or one flea or tick tucked into his hairdo.

"Whatcha think?" Doe asked. "Looking good, right?"

That's when I realized that dog was me! I turned around to sniff my back. Clean! Fresh! I didn't smell like mud or rotting leaves or dead squirrel. Instead, I smelled like, uh, uh, uh, *lavender.* I sneezed. Lisa laughed.

"Allergic to your nice smell, buddy?" Lisa asked.

She knelt down and looked me over. "You're going to make someone an amazing friend," she said. "Let's get you home."

My second time in a car didn't go quite as well as the first. I felt kinda woozy and ended up throwing up in the back seat. Nobody got mad, though. Instead, Lisa pulled the car over at the next stop and cleaned me up. She gave me fresh water and put a pill in my mouth.

"The vet said this might happen," Lisa said. She rubbed my throat and gently held my snout closed. This helped the pill slide down easily.

When we got back in, I snuggled back onto the blankets and didn't wake up until the car slowed down and we pulled into a long driveway.

"Louis, we're home!" Doe said.

I didn't know who Louis was—or, what home was—but they were so happy. This made me happy.

They got me out of the car and walked me all over the lawn. I found a small bush to pee on and a bunny to dart after.

"Gonna have to work on that!" Lisa said. "Can't just go chasing every last creature in the suburbs like you did in the woods."

Then they brought me into the house and showed me around the living room, the dining room, and my favorite spot: the sunroom. A big fluffy bed sat in the corner surrounded by tall windows. The sun streamed in bright and warm all around me. This room led to a backyard filled with trees and bushes and *lots* of squirrels and bunnies and birds. I was gonna like it here. And though Lisa and Doe were only my foster family for now, I could tell they already liked having me here.

"Being foster failures wouldn't be the *worst thing*," Doe said as she watched me sniff around the sun room.

"I know," Lisa said. "But we have to see how he does with Vincent. And if we have two dogs, then it'll be harder to foster other dogs."

"Not really," Doe said. "We can always have three…"

Lisa laughed and said, "Well, let's get the crate set up and the baby gates up. Your dad is bringing Vincent back home in an hour."

• • •

Vincent, it turns out, was Lisa and Doe's *other* dog. He was a brindle Staffordshire terrier—or maybe a mix—they didn't really know. He was much smaller than me, but had a much bigger, blockier head. When Lisa and Doe's dad split up, they decided Vincent would travel with Doe. When Doe was at Lisa's house, Vincent was at Lisa's house. When Doe went to her dad's, so did Vincent. It worked out great—especially since it meant they had a built-in dog-sitter for vacations. But whenever Lisa and Doe took in a new foster dog, Vincent had to get used to yet another animal in the house. This went well most of the time, but sometimes it was tricky.

The good news was: Vincent and I got along perfectly. In fact, we got along like we'd always lived in the same house. We chased each other in the yard and snuggled for our naps. We played tug-o-war in the house and wrestled in the backyard.

Vincent taught me a lot too—like, how to sit nicely for treats and how to walk without pulling and how to eat bite-by-bite instead of

wolfing down my food in one gulp. Vincent taught me so much, in fact, that Lisa got an idea.

"Vincent didn't pass the Helper Hounds test, but I wonder about Louis," Lisa said to Doe one day.

Doe agreed, and before I knew it, I tagged along to Vincent's obedience classes. There, I met a woman who pushed strollers and wheelchairs around me and used toys to make thunder and sirens and other loud noises. Nothing scared me, and all the tricks were easy. I did great.

So one day, Lisa sent two emails. One, to the director of the rescue she worked for. *I think we'd like to keep Louis,* she typed. And the other, to Mr. Tuttle, of Helper Hounds fame.

CHAPTER 4

You might remember me. We met years ago when Vincent came to Helper Hounds University. He famously flunked out, of course. (I still can't believe he tipped over the wheelchair!) But he's still an ace at obedience and a delight at the local library. And he's the best foster brother any dog could hope for. Lots of dogs have homes because of him. Speaking of that, we recently rescued a standard poodle—big, sweet, smart guy—who might do well…

Lisa wrote more about me and attached a few pictures. One, from the day I showed up on their porch. The next from me playing with Vincent. Then one of me getting my Canine Good Citizen award. Then, finally, one of me after my latest session with Mrs. Tramill.

Mr. Tuttle emailed back right away.

Lisa,

How could I forget Vincent! We still laugh about Fern getting flipped out of that chair. Though, I suppose it's not funny... But I'm thrilled to hear that Vincent is still doing good in the world by helping foster new animals. That's one of the best ways a dog can help!

Speaking of which, we'd love to meet your beautiful poodle. What a transformation! He looks positively regal— like King Louis indeed...

Helper Hounds University was more fun than I thought. I got to play with lots of other dogs—some who were new like me and others who came by to get refreshers. I met Spooky and King Tut when I hopped out of the car. That test was to make sure I was okay meeting strange dogs. Helper Hounds never know what we're going to run into!

After that, we rode in cars—and even on an airplane. We went through security lines and visited strangers on the street. We went into hospitals and sat by people who cried. At every turn, Mr. Tuttle watched us carefully and took notes.

Kids weren't allowed at Helper Hounds University, so Doe had to stay home with her dad. But Mr. Tuttle said Vincent could come along. Vincent wasn't allowed to join the class, but Vincent kept me company and even showed me how to flip over a wheelchair on the last day at Helper Hounds University.

I decided *not* to try it. After lots of practice and some tests, after sitting nicely and snuggling and *not tipping over wheelchairs*, Mr. Tuttle walked up to Lisa and handed her a red Helper Hounds vest.

"Amazing dog you've got here," Mr. Tuttle said. Then he looked over at Vincent who was tugging on my tail. "Actually, you've got *two* amazing dogs, but only one gets to be a Helper Hound."

Lisa clapped and bent down to hug me. Vincent never let go of my tail.

"I can't wait to tell my daughter," Lisa said. "Doe's going to be so excited!"

And she was! When Lisa texted her a picture of me in my new red Helper Hounds vest, Doe called her mom immediately and screamed "Yaaaaay!" into the phone so loudly Vincent stopped tugging on my vest.

"My friends are going to be so jealous," Doe said. "I mean, the Helper Hounds are all over YouTube. They have so many followers on social media. He's going to be famous!"

Doe was right. I got a little bit famous. When reporters heard the story of the latest Helper Hound—how I grew up wild in the woods but now looked like a king—they went nuts. We flew to Los Angeles and New York City and did lots of Zoom interviews. Photographers came by the house to take pictures of me. Videos of my "transformation" from Bear-Dog in the North Woods to Louis the Helper Hound vent viral. Everyone was crazy about my story.

But the best part of my life wasn't the famous parts. I liked it best when I was home snuggling with Vincent and Doe and Lisa—or when I was out helping people, without cameras.

So, let's get back to helping people!

CHAPTER 5

"Thank you so much for coming!" Mr. Hartnet said. "The kids are so excited. May I?"

"Pet him?" Lisa said. "Of course!"

Mr. Hartnet crouched down to scratch my shoulder. He moved his fingers up my neck and hit my tickle spot. My back leg pedaled in the air and I licked my nose.

"You found it quick!" Lisa said.

"Luck, really," Mr. Hartnet said. "Well, that and my grandmother had a standard poodle when I was a kid. Faith—that was her name— liked when we scratched her there."

Mr. Hartnet stood back up and led us into

the teachers' lounge. He offered Lisa a seat and a bottle of water. Then he got a bowl from a cabinet, filled it with water, and set it on the floor. After I took three slurps of water, Lisa said, "Down." I lay on the soft rug beneath the coffee table.

"I've never had an issue like this," Mr. Hartnet said. "Not in my nearly twenty years of teaching. I mean, kids sometimes say racist things about one another. But we're always able to address it with conversations and apologies, and then do better. This time is different."

"How so?" Lisa asked.

Mr. Hartnet shrugged. "I'm not sure. The *times* feel different. The parents are angrier— and so are the kids. We're less understanding and patient with one another. My classroom has always been a safe place—where kids can share stories about their lives. Not this year...."

Knock. Knock.

I turned toward the door and let out my softest *woof.*

"Come in!" Mr. Hartnet said.

The door opened and a boy with a mile-wide smile walked in.

"Ajani!" Mr. Hartnet said. "Come in and meet Ms. Lisa and Louis!"

"Louis!" Ajani said. "You're even fluffier in person." He crouched to pat my poofs. "Is it true these help you float in water?"

I wriggled around so Ajani could scratch me in all my favorite spots.

"It is!" said Lisa. "They keep his elbows warm too."

"We swim at my grandfather's place in Denmark," Ajani said. "The water is *cold.* Those extra fluffs would come in handy!"

"Speaking of coming in handy," Mr. Hartnet said. "Louis is here to help our class talk about what's been going on in our class."

Ajani sucked his bottom lip in and made a weird face. "You mean, about the racism? About what Brett does?"

Mr. Hartnet smiled. "Yep. About that. And about how we should be able to talk freely and kindly to one another. I'm amazed at how well you stand up to Brett. You're a real leader

Ajani. But you shouldn't have to deal with this in school—or anywhere, of course. I'm hoping Louis can help Brett see things differently. I'm hoping we can change Brett's heart and mind."

"That'd take a miracle," said Ajani.

Lisa nodded. "Well, I can't promise to change hearts and minds. Although, I have seen the Helper Hounds work miracles."

• • •

Ajani, Lisa, Mr. Hartnet, and I walked down to the classroom. The desks faced each other in pods of three. Bright rainbow-blocked rugs lined the floors. Quotes from famous people covered the walls. A huge picture of me and the other Helper Hounds was projected onto a screen at the front of the classroom.

Lisa let go of my leash and let me roam the room. I sniffed each desk.

"Sniffing for drugs?" Mr. Hartnet asked with

a smile.

"Goodness no!" Lisa said. "Sniffing for peanut butter sandwiches, more like it."

Lisa was right. I *was* looking for PB&Js. I drooled just at the thought of finding a fresh PB&J tucked into a desk. Since most classrooms were nut-free, I hadn't smelled one in a desk or backpack in months. So instead, I just took delight in sniffing *all* the different student smells. These were fifth graders. Any Helper Hound will tell you fifth graders smell *amazing*. Bits of mud and grass stain mixed with fresh air and sweaty armpits, over-ripe bananas and yogurt. They are the best.

"Louis, here," Lisa called.

I trotted to the front of the classroom as Mr. Hartnet pointed out the quotes around the room.

"I try to set up my classroom to build community and unity," Mr. Hartnet said. "I like to see my students work together and help each other. This year has been a struggle."

"The worst was when he made fun of Rosa Parks during history," said Ajani. "Brett said, 'Maybe if she spoke Danish, they would've let her ride in the front of the bus!'"

Ajani shook his head. "I know people say ugly things, because they're angry or stupid —sorry, because they don't *know* better. But not all the kids know that. And Brett says bad things about all of us—the Black kids, the Asian kids, the Mexican kids. It's terrible!"

Mr. Hartnet put his arm around Ajani's shoulders and said, "All the kids look up to you for how you stand up to Brett. You're brave and a real leader. Are you brave enough to introduce Louis to your classmates?"

Ajani smiled and nodded. "Sure," he said. "In which language?"

The humans all laughed. I was more focused

on the rumble of footsteps heading toward the classroom. Moments later, twenty students filed into the room. Some gasped when they saw me. Others rushed to greet me. Still others walked slowly around.

One boy looked wide-eyed and smiled brightly. He stopped just past the doorway as another boy pushed past him.

"Ah," Mr. Hartnet said quietly. "That's Brett pushing in."

Brett stopped dead in his tracks when he saw me. I wagged my tail at him, but he went right to his seat. Other kids gathered around to pet me and ask Lisa questions. As they did, I stood straighter and let the poof of my tail ride extra high.

Ajani leaned down to pet my neck and tell one girl about me. As he did, Brett yelled out: "Ajani, that dog has a big afro just like you. Maybe you're Jamaican, Danish, *and* poodle!"

Two boys around Brett laughed. Ajani glared
at Brett and started to speak. But Lisa spoke
first.

"Well, poodles come in a variety of colors,
including apricot," Lisa said. "Looking at your
lovely reddish curls, perhaps that's what you
would be: An *apricot* poodle!"

Ajani smiled. The boys around Brett laughed again. This time, with fingers pointed at him. He told them to shut up before Lisa continued.

"But as we'll all learn, a poodle would be a great dog to be: they are some of the smartest, most athletic dogs around. And this doesn't matter if they are apricot, *blue*, black, brown, cream, white, *sable*, or silver. They're all athletic and brainiacs."

"If they're brainiacs," one of the boys said, "Brett *definitely* isn't a poodle."

"All right, class," Mr. Hartnet said as he clapped his hands. "Let's get seated and settle down as we officially welcome our guests, Miss Lisa and Louis, the Helper Hound."

The students all clapped and sat in their seats. Ajani read the intro about the Helper Hounds in general and talked about me in specific. Then Lisa began the slideshow.

CHAPTER 6

"We're going to be dog detectives," she said. "I want you to tell me what you observe about the dogs I show you."

A picture of me sniffing around the cabin porch appeared on the screen.

"Is it even a dog?" one girl said. "Looks like a bear."

"He *does* look like a bear," Lisa said. "But no. It's not a bear. But what does his bear-likeness tell you about this dog? About his story?"

"It looks lost," a boy said. "And sad. He's got all that stuff in his fur."

"He looks like he has a bad life," one girl

said. "Like no one loves him. He will probably get rabies or bite someone because he's wild and doesn't know how to be nice to people. Maybe he'll have to get put down."

I shuddered at the thought!

"That's awful!" a boy said.

"Yes, that would be," said Lisa.

She clicked ahead to the next slide. A picture of Vincent popped up. He was jumping in the air. His tight muscles bulged. His brindle fur stood straight up. His mouth was wide open and his teeth gleamed as they got ready to chomp down on the tennis ball in the air.

"That dog looks *crazy*!" a boy said. "Like he's about to attack someone."

"Okay," Lisa said. "So, tell me about *his* life."

"I bet he spends his days chained outside so when he's loose, he can't wait to attack things."

Lisa nodded. "Very good. Dogs kept on chains can get angry. But now, let's look at this dog."

Lisa flashed another picture of Vincent on the screen. This time, Vincent snuggled up next to a five-year-old at the library.

"Tell me about *this* dog," Lisa said. "Any clues in this picture to tell you about his life?"

The students called out different answers:

"He looks nice."

"He looks like people love him."

"He looks cuddly."

Lisa nodded along as each student added something.

"Is he a Helper Hound?" Ajani asked. "He looks familiar."

"Nice!" Lisa said. "He's actually *not* a Helper Hound—"

Before she could finish, Brett interrupted with laughter.

"...*But*," Lisa said. "That's Vincent, Louis's brother! And this is the same dog you saw in the other picture. Vincent wasn't about to bite someone—just about to catch a tennis ball. Anyway, Vincent tried to become a Helper Hound but kept pushing over wheelchairs.

Sooooooo, today, he helps kids in school with their reading."

"Vincent teaches kids to read—and reading teaches us to change the world!" Mr. Hartnet said. "Well done, Vincent!"

"But, what about the first dog? The bear dog? Do we see another picture of him?" a girl asked.

"Well," Lisa said. "I don't have another picture of him."

The class sighed.

"Because the bear dog is right here!" Lisa said. "That's Louis on the day we first met him."

"No way!" Ajani said. He smiled at me and shook his head. "You looked *rough*, buddy."

"He was! So what does this tell us about our dog-detective skills?" Lisa asked.

The class went quiet. I followed a small fly that buzzed around my head.

Finally, one kid said: "We stink at it."

It was Brett. Lisa smiled and said, "Good.

That's right. Anybody else? What does it say
about what we can tell about someone or
something's life just by looking at them?"

Ajani looked right at me, smiled, and said:
"We learned it's hard to tell a dog's life story
from one picture or even just the way they
look."

"Good! Yes!" Lisa said. "We can tell *lots* of things about dogs from what we see. We can read their body language to see if they're relaxed or happy or nervous. And we can tell how they've been cared for. But we don't know everything. It's the same with people."

"Think about that picture of Vincent," Mr. Hartnet said. "He looked *vicious!*"

"Right," said Lisa. "And, to be honest, some people think he *is* mean because he is a pit bull. Sometimes people cross the street because they are scared. But look at that picture. Vincent is a cuddle bug!"

"Unless you're a tennis ball," Brett said.

The boys around him laughed. So did Ajani. But I was too distracted to notice. The fly buzzed and buzzed all around me. I lifted my snout into the air to see if I could reach it. No luck. The fly stayed *just* out of reach.

I stopped watching the fly when I heard my

name.

"Louis looks like he is from somewhere very fancy—like Paris," one girl said. "It funny to think he wandered around the woods like a bear."

"But maybe instead of finding that funny," Lisa said, "we can find it *interesting*. I mean, everyone is full of surprises! We all have weird things in our past or about ourselves. That's why making new friends is so fun. People are mysteries. We spoil the fun of getting to know one another when we think we know everything based on what we *look* like. There are so many better ways to get to know people."

Lisa put up a picture of Mrs. Tramill and told the class about how she was the best educated dog groomer in the world. "Now, it sometimes sounds like bragging," Lisa said. "But really, Mrs. Tramill just wants to be *known*—and she likes to surprise people. Nobody thinks you go to Harvard to groom poodles. But it's fun to discover this part of her story."

"I wonder what we can discover about one another," Mr. Hartnet said. He began a small lecture on the ways they can get to know one another. They can ask questions, he said. They can listen to stories. They can eat at each other's houses and try new food. The list went on and on, but I was barely listening.

The fly continued to hound me. It landed on my poofs and on my shaved spots. It flew around my ears and eyes. I began to have flashbacks to my days in the woods. I shivered as I remembered the way all those other bugs used to bite me.

And then, the fly landed right on my nose. If only it would fly just a little lower. Then, maybe I could…

Chomp!

The fly passed in front of my long snout

and I took action. I clamped my mouth shut.
I had it! The fly zipped around the inside of
my mouth. So I swallowed. Hard. That's when
things went very wrong.

CHAPTER 7

Brett was the first to notice. I gagged and gagged. My tongue hung out of my mouth. The fly had gone down my throat and gotten stuck. It bounced around the inside of me. I shook and shook and gagged and gagged. But the fly did not budge. A bitter taste rose from down deep, and I struggled to breathe.

"Louis!" Brett said. "He needs help!"

Ajani flew out of his desk chair. Lisa squatted next to me.

"I saw him watching that fly," Brett said. "I think he ate it."

"Everyone, please stay in your seats," Mr.

Hartnet said.

Ajani ignored Mr. Hartnet.

"I can help," Ajani said. "My grandpa's a goat farmer."

I didn't know what being a goat farmer had to do with me. But in one smooth motion, Ajani reached his arms around me. He moved his balled-up fists under my rib cage and squeezed. Once. Twice. And then—blech! The fly flew

out! Well, dropped out, would be more like it. When flies are covered in dog spit, they drop to the floor.

I shook my whole body. Then I turned around to slurp Ajani. He saved my life! At least, that's what it felt like.

Lisa thanked Ajani and the whole class cheered. Brett quietly slid the slobbery fly onto a sheet of paper and tapped it out an open window.

"Fly free," Brett whispered.

Brett walked over and patted my top poof. He told me I was a good boy.

"Cool that you know about saving goats and dogs," Brett said to Ajani.

"Cool that you saved that fly," Ajani said.

The boys fist-bumped, and then both returned to petting me.

Brett shrugged. "I don't like when animals die or get hurt…"

"Me neither," Ajani said.

Obviously, I didn't mind when flies got hurt, but I slurped Brett's hand. He may have said mean things in the past. But when people are trying to be better, it's good to reward them.

"Okay," Mr. Hartnet said. "Let's let Louis get a slurp of water and catch his breath. The rest of us can take a moment and ask our pod-mates a question about their lives. I put some examples on the board. Let's surprise each other!"

Lisa fetched my water bowl from the Helper Hounds sack. Mr. Hartnet motioned to Brett and Ajani that they could stay by me. As Lisa set the bowl in front of me and poured water into it, Brett looked at Ajani. Ajani looked back. I slurped up the water and then booped both boys with my wet snout.

"Gross," they both said at the same time.

Brett smiled and then said, "That's, uh,

interesting that your grandpa is a farmer. My
uncle is a farmer too. He has sheep, mostly,
but a few goats to cut the lawn. He lives in
Wisconsin. Do your grandpa's goats live in
Denmark?"

"In Jamaica," Ajani said. "My grandfather in
Denmark doesn't have goats. But, uh, he gets

mice in his apartment. And *mice* in Danish sounds like *moose*. So it sounds like he has *moose* in his apartment."

Ajani cracked a smile. Then Brett laughed—loudly! Soon both boys were cracking up.

"The best is that he usually says a bad word when he talks about the *mus*," Ajani said. "It makes it even funnier."

Brett raised his eyebrows and leaned in. "What's *that* word? The *bad* one?"

"I don't think so, boys," Lisa said. "We're not here to help you learn bad words. But here, Louis can teach you a new word."

Both boys tilted their heads. Lisa smiled and told me to speak. I woofed my best woof. That's as bad as my words get.

Mr. Hartnet told the class to thank me and Lisa for coming. Ajani and Brett were the only two who didn't clap their thanks. But that was okay. They were still laughing together.

EPILOGUE

Dear Louis:

Catch any flies lately? Haha. Brett told me to say that. Anyway, just wanted you to know that things are going better in class! We're in a "Race in America" unit, and Mr. Hartnet makes us talk a lot. He asks questions about our backgrounds and our experiences. We've had lots of time to talk about history and tell stories about today and how things "make us feel." Sometimes that's difficult, but it's good.

I've learned lots of interesting things about my classmates—even Brett. Especially Brett.

By the way, Brett said he was sorry for making fun of me speaking Danish. My grandpa (the one with the moose in his apartment—hahaha) sent a video of some of his neighbors. One neighbor was from India, another from Japan, one from Indiana, and another from Ethiopia. They all spoke Danish. Brett never laughed once. Well, except when he wondered if they had said any bad words about "mus." I laughed at that too.

Did you ever see moose when you lived in the woods? I wish I would've asked that.

Anyway, I better go. Brett and his family are coming over for some of my mom's famous jerk chicken. Of course, Brett thinks "jerk" is hilarious. But that's okay. It'll be even funnier when he takes a bite and sees how spicy it is!

Oh, my mom just read this and said that was mean. But, she's smiling too. Hope to see you again soon!

Love,

Ajani

Louis's
Tips for Overcoming Racism

Racism is the belief that one race (group of people based on skin color) is better than another.

Being proud of where your family is from or loving your family more than others is not racist. That's normal! It's okay for me to be proud that I'm a standard poodle and to love my black curly hair. It's not okay for me to think Vincent isn't as good as me because his hair is straight and striped. It's like that for people, too. Racism is thinking people who look or sound like you are better than those who don't.

No one is born racist. People learn to behave this way. Sometimes they learn it from their families. Sometimes they learn it from people in power. Sometimes they learn it from stuff they read or from other kids. But we can learn to be *anti-racist* (that means: we can learn to fight racism like Ajani!) in many ways:

Study different cultures. The more I learn about other animals, the more I like them. Same is true for people. I study people by sniffing them. You can study people by reading books, traveling, trying different foods, or doing some of these other tips.

Hang out with people from different backgrounds.
When we get to know people or animals who
are different from us and when we listen to
their stories, we become kinder. We learn to
find each other interesting—and not weird or
scary. Lisa likes to read books and listen to
music or watch movies made by people from
different backgrounds or different countries.
This also helps us understand different
experiences.

Speak up. When you hear someone say
something mean or use an ugly word
about a person of a different race,
say something. This can feel
scary—especially if it is
an adult saying it. But
it's important to let the
person know those
words hurt people.

About Standard Poodles

You can tell from the story that Louis is a smart dog. In fact, Poodles are one of the smartest breeds of dogs. These dogs are great athletes too! There's a lot to love about this breed.

When it comes to Poodles, one size doesn't fit all. Dog experts recognize three different varieties. Standard Poodles, like Louis, are the biggest. They are more than 15 inches tall and can weigh up to 70 pounds. Miniature Poodles are between 10 and 15 inches tall. Toy Poodles are the smallest. They are no more than 10 inches tall.

One of the most amazing things about Poodles is their fur. Poodle fur is super-thick and super-curly. It's no wonder people thought Louis looked like a bear before he found a good family to take care of him.

It's important to keep a Poodle's fur under control. Many people bring their dogs to groomers for a special haircut. The classic Poodle cut includes shaving the fur on the dog's legs, neck, and tail. The fur on the lower legs, chest, hips,

and the tip of the tail stays long. These long puffs of fur are called pompons.

There is an important reason for the Poodle's odd hairstyle. More than 400 years ago, these dogs were used to help hunters retrieve ducks from the water. Poodles are great water dogs because they are very strong and athletic, and they are fantastic swimmers too. So what does that have to do with how the Poodle's fur is trimmed? Hunters wanted the dog to be able to swim easily, but they also needed a way to keep the dog warm in the cold water. So they left the fur long where the dog needed it most to stay warm.

Many people think the Poodle originally came from France. Nope! The dog is originally from Germany. The word "Poodle" comes from a German word, "pudelin," which means "splashing in water." However, Poodles became very popular in France. They became the favorite companions of kings and queens. Today, Poodles are the national dog of France.

We mentioned that Poodles are very smart. These dogs are good at learning tricks. In the past, they were often featured in circuses, where they would balance on wires and do many different acrobatic acts. Today, these dogs are great at obedience and agility trials and can also make excellent therapy dogs and companions.

HELPER HOUNDS

If you loved reading about Louis, you should discover the other seven Helper Hounds!

Check with your favorite bookstore or library